Let's Go, Seahawks!

Aimee Aryal

Illustrated by Miguel De Angel

SEATTLE
SEAHAWKS

MASCOT
BOOKS®
www.mascotbooks.com

It was a beautiful fall day in the Pacific Northwest. Seattle Seahawks fans from all over the area were on their way to Qwest Field to watch their Seahawks play football.

All over town, everyone dressed in Seahawks colors. As fans made their way to the stadium, they cheered, "Let's go, Seahawks!"

Hours before the start of the game, fans began gathering at "Touchdown City" in the Qwest Field Event Center. Children played games and watched Blitz entertain Seahawks fans. Some children, and even a few adults, painted their faces for the game!

As fans walked through the
Qwest Field gates, they cheered,
"Let's go, Seahawks!"

The team gathered in the locker room before the game. Players strapped on their pads and dressed in their Seattle Seahawks uniforms.

The coach delivered final instructions and encouraged the team to play their best. The coach cheered, "Let's go, Seahawks!"

It was now time for the Seattle Seahawks to take the field. The announcer called, "Ladies and gentlemen, please welcome your Seattle Seahawks!" The Seahawks sprinted onto the field and were greeted by their loyal fans. It was very loud in the stadium!

The Seahawks huddled around the team captains and cheered, "Let's go, Seahawks!"

The team captains met at midfield for the coin toss. The referee flipped a coin high in the air and the visiting team called, "Heads." The coin landed with the heads side up – the Seahawks would begin the game by kicking off.

The referee reminded the players that it was important to play hard, but also with good sportsmanship.

The Seahawks kicker booted the ball down the field to start the action. With the game underway, the kicker cheered, "Let's go, Seahawks!"

After the opening kickoff, it was time for
the Seahawks defense to take the field. Blitz
led the crowd in a "DE-FENSE" chant. One fan
held up a "D" in one hand and a picket fence
in the other. With the crowd's encouragement,
the Seahawks defense broke through and
sacked the quarterback. Fans appreciated the
great play and cheered, "Let's go, Seahawks!"

After the defense did its job, the Seahawks offense went to work. With great teamwork, they marched down the field. On fourth down, the team was only one yard away from the end zone.

"Let's go for it!" instructed the coach, and the quarterback called a play in the huddle.

The quarterback yelled, "Down. Set. Hike!" before handing the ball to the running back, who crossed the goal line.

TOUCHDOWN!

After the score, the crowd erupted with joy and fans cheered, "Let's go, Seahawks!"

At the end of the first half, the Seahawks headed back to the locker room. The coach stopped to answer a few questions from a television reporter. In the locker room, the team rested and prepared for the second half.

Meanwhile, Seahawks fans stretched their legs and picked up a few snacks at the concession stands. In the concourse, Seahawks fans cheered, "Let's go, Seahawks!"

In the second half, the temperature dropped
and rain began to fall. The team played hard
through the storm. Young Seahawks fans drank
hot chocolate to help them stay warm. One
little fan was surprised to see herself on the big
screen. With everybody watching, she cheered,
"Let's go, Seahawks!"

With only a few seconds remaining, the score was tied. The Seahawks lined-up for a field goal try. After a good snap and a perfect hold, the kicker booted the ball toward the goal posts. The stadium was nearly silent as all eyes followed the flight of the ball.

The kick was good!

The Seattle Seahawks won the football game! The kicker cheered, "Let's go, Seahawks!"

To celebrate the thrilling victory, Seahawks players dumped water on the coach. The teams shook hands and congratulated each other on a good game. As Seahawks fans left Qwest Field, they cheered, "Let's go, Seahawks!"

For Anna and Maya. ~ Aimee Aryal

For Sue, Ana Milagros, and Angel Miguel. ~ Miguel De Angel

www.seahawks.com

For more information, please contact Mascot Books,
P.O. Box 220157, Chantilly, VA 20153-0157

SEAHAWKS, SEATTLE SEAHAWKS, and BLITZ
are trademarks or registered trademarks of Football Northwest, LLC.

ISBN: 978-1-932888-95-9

Printed in the United States.

www.mascotbooks.com

Title List

Team	Book Title	Author
Baseball		
Boston Red Sox	Hello, Wally!	Jerry Remy
Boston Red Sox	Wally And His Journey Through Red Sox Nation!	Jerry Remy
New York Yankees	Let's Go, Yankees!	Yogi Berra
New York Mets	Hello, Mr. Met!	Rusty Staub
St. Louis Cardinals	Hello, Fredbird!	Ozzie Smith
Philadelphia Phillies	Hello, Phillie Phanatic!	Aimee Aryal
Chicago Cubs	Let's Go, Cubs!	Aimee Aryal
Chicago White Sox	Let's Go, White Sox!	Aimee Aryal
Cleveland Indians	Hello, Slider!	Bob Feller
College		
Alabama	Hello, Big Al!	Aimee Aryal
Alabama	Roll Tide!	Ken Stabler
Arizona	Hello, Wilbur!	Lute Olsen
Arkansas	Hello, Big Red!	Aimee Aryal
Auburn	Hello, Aubie!	Aimee Aryal
Auburn	War Eagle!	Pat Dye
Boston College	Hello, Baldwin!	Aimee Aryal
Brigham Young	Hello, Cosmo!	LaVell Edwards
Clemson	Hello, Tiger!	Aimee Aryal
Colorado	Hello, Ralphie!	Aimee Aryal
Connecticut	Hello, Jonathan!	Aimee Aryal
Duke	Hello, Blue Devil!	Aimee Aryal
Florida	Hello, Albert!	Aimee Aryal
Florida State	Let's Go, 'Noles!	Aimee Aryal
Georgia	Hello, Hairy Dawg!	Aimee Aryal
Georgia	How 'Bout Them Dawgs!	Vince Dooley
Georgia Tech	Hello, Buzz!	Aimee Aryal
Illinois	Let's Go, Illini!	Aimee Aryal
Indiana	Let's Go, Hoosiers!	Aimee Aryal
Iowa	Hello, Herky!	Aimee Aryal
Iowa State	Hello, Cy!	Amy DeLashmutt
James Madison	Hello, Duke Dog!	Aimee Aryal
Kansas	Hello, Big Jay!	Aimee Aryal
Kansas State	Hello, Willie!	Dan Walter
Kentucky	Hello, Wildcat!	Aimee Aryal
Louisiana State	Hello, Mike!	Aimee Aryal
Maryland	Hello, Testudo!	Aimee Aryal
Michigan	Let's Go, Blue!	Aimee Aryal
NBA		
Dallas Mavericks	Let's Go, Mavs!	Mark Cuban
Kentucky Derby		
Kentucky Derby	White Diamond Runs For The Roses	Aimee Aryal

Team	Book Title	Author
Pro Football		
Carolina Panthers	Let's Go, Panthers!	Aimee Aryal
Dallas Cowboys	How 'Bout Them Cowboys!	Aimee Aryal
Green Bay Packers	Go, Packres, Go!	Aimee Aryal
Kansas City Chiefs	Let's Go, Chiefs!	Aimee Aryal
Minnesota Vikings	Let's Go, Vikings!	Aimee Aryal
New York Giants	Let's Go, Giants!	Aimee Aryal
New England Patriots	Let's Go, Patriots!	Aimee Aryal
Seattle Seahawks	Let's Go, Seahawks!	Aimee Aryal
Washington Redskins	Hail To The Redskins!	Aimee Aryal
Coloring Book		
Dallas Cowboys	How 'Bout Them Cowboys!	Aimee Aryal
Michigan State	Hello, Sparty!	Aimee Aryal
Minnesota	Hello, Goldy!	Aimee Aryal
Mississippi	Hello, Colonel Rebel!	Aimee Aryal
Mississippi State	Hello, Bully!	Aimee Aryal
Missouri	Hello, Truman!	Todd Donoho
Nebraska	Hello, Herbie Husker!	Aimee Aryal
North Carolina	Hello, Rameses!	Aimee Aryal
North Carolina St.	Hello, Mr. Wuf!	Aimee Aryal
Notre Dame	Let's Go, Irish!	Aimee Aryal
Ohio State	Hello, Brutus!	Aimee Aryal
Oklahoma	Let's Go, Sooners!	Aimee Aryal
Oklahoma State	Hello, Pistol Pete!	Aimee Aryal
Penn State	Hello, Nittany Lion!	Aimee Aryal
Penn State	We Are Penn State!	Joe Paterno
Purdue	Hello, Purdue Pete!	Aimee Aryal
Rutgers	Hello, Scarlet Knight!	Aimee Aryal
South Carolina	Hello, Cocky!	Aimee Aryal
So. California	Hello, Tommy Trojan!	Aimee Aryal
Syracuse	Hello, Otto!	Aimee Aryal
Tennessee	Hello, Smokey!	Aimee Aryal
Texas	Hello, Hook 'Em!	Aimee Aryal
Texas A & M	Howdy, Reveille!	Aimee Aryal
UCLA	Hello, Joe Bruin!	Aimee Aryal
Virginia	Hello, CavMan!	Aimee Aryal
Virginia Tech	Hello, Hokie Bird!	Aimee Aryal
Virginia Tech	Yea, It's Hokie Game Day!	Frank Beamer
Wake Forest	Hello, Demon Deacon!	Aimee Aryal
West Virginia	Hello, Mountaineer!	Aimee Aryal
Wisconsin	Hello, Bucky!	Aimee Aryal

More great titles coming soon!

info@mascotbooks.com